The Mouse and the Grouse

Written by
Gregory Franklin Huyette

Illustrated by
Vanessa Richardson

The teeny, tiny mouse
said to the finely feathered grouse,
"I'd like to come and visit you
in your lofty, lovely house."

The finely feathered grouse
smiled at the teeny, tiny mouse
And said, "You can't since I'm saving it
for my future spouse."

The sad teeny, tiny mouse said,
  as tears started to douse,
"I'm lonely and just wanted to say hello,
  finely feathered grouse."

Well, the finely feathered grouse
with his lofty, lovely house
Was lonely too since he hadn't
yet found his future spouse.

But how could a mouse so teeny, tiny
and a grouse so fine of feather
Ever visit each other
and have a talk together?

They had nothing in common
and their lives had different starts.
Although one thing was the same;
they both had hurting hearts.

No one had ever visited
the finely feathered grouse
And he did like the friendly words
uttered by the teeny, tiny mouse.

As mister mouse gazed aloft,
sir grouse returned that smile
And suddenly blurted out,
"Come on up and we'll chat for awhile."

Overjoyed, the teeny, tiny mouse jumped,
but just bumped the tree.
Then tears wet ears to tail
as teeny moaned mournfully,

"You can fly free through the air,
but alas, I'm earthbound.
There's no hope since you live in a tree,
but my house is on the ground."

Suddenly, a star
from the heavens
flashed an idea
for these two.

Perhaps they
could visit together
if both tried
something new.

The finely feathered grouse
left his lofty, lovely house
And eagerly landed in a bush
near the star struck tiny mouse.

In one hop teeny, tiny leapt toward the bush
and I've heard tell,

That the friendship of grouse and mouse
has been doing very well.

Dedicated with eternal love to McKenna, Samantha and Jack plus baby boy Sas and baby girl Benadom, both in transit between heaven and earth. These wonderful grandchildren are the promise of a bright future!

-G.F.H.

Text Copyright © 2006 by Gregory Franklin Huyette
Illustration Copyright © 2006 VR Illustration

Happy Books Press
Agoura, California

The Mouse and the Grouse
Summary:
Although different in many ways the Teeny Tiny Mouse and the Finely Feathered Grouse had things in common like loneliness and the need for friends. The Mouse and the Grouse became real friends because each changed their ways to help the other.

ISBN-10 0-9787826-0-7
ISBN-13 9-780978-782603
First Edition 2006
Printed and bound in China